Penguin Books
The Saddest Summer of

J. P. Donleavy was born in New York City in
1926 and educated there and at Trinity College,
Dublin. In addition to *The Saddest Summer of
Samuel S*, his works include the novels, *The
Ginger Man*, *A Singular Man*, *The Beastly
Beatitudes of Balthazar B*, *The Onion Eaters*,
*A Fairy Tale of New York* and *The Destinies of
Darcy Dancer, Gentleman*; a book of short
pieces, *Meet My Maker The Mad Molecule*;
and four plays, *The Ginger Man*, *Fairy Tales of
New York*, *A Singular Man* and *The Saddest
Summer of Samuel S* (published in Penguins
under the title *The Plays of J. P. Donleavy*);
and *The Unexpurgated Code: A Complete
Manual of Survival and Manners* (1975).

J. P. Donleavy

# The Saddest Summer
# of Samuel S

Penguin Books
in association with Eyre & Spottiswoode

Penguin Books Ltd, Harmondsworth,
Middlesex, England
Penguin Books, 625 Madison Avenue, New York,
New York 10022, U.S.A.
Penguin Books Australia Ltd, Ringwood,
Victoria, Australia
Penguin Books Canada Ltd, 2801 John Street,
Markham, Ontario, Canada L3R 1B4
Penguin Books (N.Z.) Ltd, 182–190 Wairau Road,
Auckland 10, New Zealand

First published in the U.S.A. 1966
Published in Great Britain by Eyre & Spottiswoode 1967
Published in Penguin Books 1968
Reprinted 1972, 1974, 1976, 1979

Made and printed in Great Britain by
Hazell Watson & Viney Ltd, Aylesbury, Bucks
Set in Linotype Georgian

He lived in a grey shadowy street in Vienna two flights up behind four dirt stained never opened windows. He rose slowly mornings paddling off balance on bare feet to the dark stale air of his bathroom across the hall. Sometimes pausing to watch the little line of red ants disappearing down into the wall. He had arrived at an age when the flesh begins to go its own way and the spirit struggles to hold it back.

He took good care of his heart by eating the boiled meats and never let religion rob him of his appetite or sense of humour. Life was still before him in this strange outpost of a city where the sounds of the rest of the world drifted and one had to tap one's skull to let them in. Five years ago he had a plan to straighten himself out and now these many thousands of dollars later he still went, clocking in twice a week to this small rotund doctor who sat askance in the shadows quietly listening and sometimes chuckling. And at long last he had an insight. That one grows old faster staying in the same place.

Samuel S had devised a rhythm of life and a trickle of income, setting up little projects which could last him, if not the rest of his life at least six weeks at a stretch. He became a specialist in American hospitality, collecting three female clients of Vienna's old world who felt a whimsical need to keep up with the new. After their second little get together with hominy cakes and a re-enactment of a Harvard president's tea, he abruptly wore out his welcome and temporary profession by crossing his legs with the topmost knee under a tray of Dresden. There were embarrassing stains on two of his clients' dresses. The third client further busting up his party and her own friendships by doubling up with laughter and falling on the floor where she rolled. This latter client, a widowed countess, went on to lesson three, the lighting of a match on the sole of one's boot. She thought this great stuff and Samuel S suspected she was out for laughs and like his analyst was tuning an ear, albeit elegant, to his remarks and chuckling just enough so that he could not plant a kiss there as well.

The Countess, light haired and willowy with wiry muscle, maintained that it was monstrous that a man of Samuel S's sensibility, wit and knowledge, should go to waste on the world. And upon these occasions Samuel S would say, 'Ah but Countess, you appreciate me and that is enough.'

'Ah that is so Herr S and I am flattered that you should feel so.'

And so Samuel S skied down the spiritual slopes towards the buds of May and this continental summer. With an odd dipping of a ski pole in a deep depression. But attending the Opera, nights of Mozart and Verdi, the Countess taking his arm as they slowly made their way up to the foyer where under the gleaming chandeliers she told him who was not quite who but who they thought they were. Twice it got tense as they returned to her apartments and she said there is seven years between us Herr S because I do not lie about my age, but perhaps I should lie because I could. And then she left him standing there on this sombre sandal wood scented landing with the door slowly closing in his face. And the second time she had said 'Come in, come in.' She played Fauré's Requiem on her gramophone and poured him a viertel of champagne in a tumbler and Samuel S thought, this is it, I've broken through the culture and will soon have her in the bedroom. But she said in a loud clear voice, 'What on earth is the matter with us, Herr S we are living in some kind of phoney dream world, who cares if we go to the opera, who cares if we are superiors in this village which used to be a city.' And she smiled, warm and wan. 'Ah Herr S it would be so nice if we could waste time on the bank of some river back in my young days while thinking there was a lifetime to be lived.'

Samuel S reserved this disconcerting thought to pass on to the Herr Doctor and he put a straight question to him. 'Herr Doctor do you think this Countess is giving me the runaround. I mean to say she must need it.' Herr Doctor with a gentle finger scratched a little area under his eye and said what he always said, 'Please continue.' These were cold words during an even colder winter in Austria when the rooftops wore white for weeks and chimneys melted snow by day and at night left a streak of ice which gleamed in the sun at dawn. Then slowly, with much warning, his money ran out. And Samuel S went silently under. Skis, poles and all. Deep down. Just as the sappy tips of buds were sneaking out on the trees the centre of April.

He went foolishly from one acquaintance to another for palmfuls of coins. Until a chill crept up the backs of his legs and he dragged his heels through the streets. And late one afternoon the end of May and in the middle of a tiny deserted square, three ghosts stood in the entrances of the three alleys ahead, one said I am poverty and bring lonely sickness, another said nothing but broke mystical wind and the last, a Radcliffe girl said, although she only wore red and blue striped ankle socks she had graduated. Samuel S stopped, shivered and made for the nearest post office where he bought a telegram and cried out desperately to rich friends in Amsterdam to send money, a bulk sum, to hold him afloat because he was sinking, sinking.

And Samuel S sank. The money arrived. But not before his rent was in arrears and the police came and took his passport away. The day he slapped down the bills in front of the twitching landlord's nose and retrieved his passport, he was evicted. He stood on the street waiting for a taxi as the landlord, making the sign of the cross, padlocked the door behind him. At the Südbahnholf he checked his possessions ready for trains south to Venice, Trieste or Istanbul and phoned the Countess. And she said don't go, call me back in ten minutes, I have an impecunious friend, a widow like myself who has three spare rooms.

In twenty minutes he had a new landlady.

He presented himself from the station. To this widow, aristocratic, nosey and no longer living in the best part of town, he bowed, she smiled. She had hair, she had breasts and legs as well. They settled down nicely as landlady and tenant. While there was a brief equestrian spell taking the Countess riding in the Prater, where once she pulled her horse up under a tree, her blonde hair flying and said, 'Herr S there is one thing about you which is impressive, you never let your demeanour brag.'

For three weeks two days he had a breather and slowly hauled himself out of the abyss. Passing daily across the tiles of his landing, a yellow towel wrapped at his throat, boots gleaming, spurs jangling, snapping a willow branch against his thigh. In the Prater they cantered under the branches. Inhaling the deep green fuming from the trees. Then wham. The Countess drew up her horse again under her same favourite tree and there in the midweek of his awaking chipperness let him have a bolo to the plexus.

'Herr S you ride brilliantly. But I think enough is enough, don't you.'

Samuel S saved the look on his face all the way back to his chambers. Plopped down in his dusty chair legs akimbo. He was cruel to his horse, slamming the bit back into its jaws. The Countess was trying to shoot him down, as women did when he outcooked, outrode, outspoke them and they would not lay. Now put his riding gear into mothballs, along with his course on American hospitality, phonetics, great paintings, semantics and his will to go on fighting. Until he heard the slippered shufflings. The landlady with her ear to the door. And he quietly levered himself up out of his seat and put his ear there as well and then his eye to the keyhole. Eye to eye, one thing did not quite lead to another, but enough so that some weeks later at ten thirty of a morning she might knock.

'Herr S.'

'Was ist.'

'Herr S, excuse me this morning.'

'I excused you yesterday morning.'

'Again excuse me this morning.'

These exchanges were a preamble to their little get togethers which ended up in a fierce race around his dining room table. She was in good condition and impossible to catch. Finally as she stood there huffing and puffing, while he was near apoplectic, she would agree to a compromise.

'Herr Sam I will stand here on this side of the table if you stand on that side of the table.'

Sam S stood on his side of the table. Her eyes narrowed when she smiled. With two front teeth replaced. She stood naked from the waist up as he stood naked from the waist down, conducting among other things a foolish conversation across the dregs of his breakfast. The tram outside below shuddering the double paned windows as the steel wheels ground over the gravel thrown on the tracks. This was the routine which had developed and been cultivated until he found a name to say to her across the table.

'Agnes Anxiety.'

'Herr Sam don't call me that.'

'Why can't we have a normal sexual relationship.'

'You frighten me, Herr S.'

'Wow. I frighten you. Do you know Agnes you frighten me. But if this is what God is giving me for my recreation, I'm not religious enough to ask for a change.'

The landlady always took time to chew over his remarks, her lips grinning as she tried to peer into the dark cave of this half man, half beast, two thirds gentleman who did not add up, standing ample bellied on the other side of the mahogany. And her voice would have a soft friendliness as she needled into his life.

'Herr Sam your brain thinks too much.'

'And it's thinking right now why you don't get into bed with me. At our age this is disaster.'

'Herr Sam what do you do in the rooms these times when you do not leave for three days.'

'I think.'

'What do you think.'

'What do you think.'

'I think you was crazy.'

'Please continue, Agnes Anxiety.'

'Why do you live in Vienna.'

'So that when the time comes for suicide I will have no qualms leaving the Viennese to clean up the remains.'

'Shame.'

'But to their eternal credit, the Viennese are not Swiss.'

'Although I am not in the habit of saying gesundheit, I say gesundheit Herr S, it is true at least we are not Swiss.'

These encounters took the mind off one's pains in the personal plumbing. And the odd mysterious throbbings in the groin which made one sail into dreamland at night just as hopeless as when sailing around the table trying to manage a grip of Agnes's backside, which in its amplitude lagged behind on the sharp turns. Then the despairing minutes sitting empty handed after she sneaked back into her own flat, as one big bright desert lay out across the folded freckled hands. A voice whispering from the horizon. Hello there, you, when will you ever be cured, be cured, be cured. Then to the window to listen to the booming sad toll of St Stephen's Cathedral bell and to see if the sun had come up once more. And want more than ever to sail into old age on an ocean liner full of bullion.

Samuel S wore his jacket on all occasions. Kept his tie knotted in position at his detached white collar atop a pin striped shirt. He sealed off the windows of his room to hold out the dirt and screeching trams down in the street. Playing it cool waltzing down the pavement like an iceberg, all loneliness under the waves. His mother nor the world cared. And when he played with a friend as a child, the friend said if I told my mother I didn't believe in God she would drop dead and Samuel S ran home, his mother was ironing in the kitchen and he said 'Hey Ma, I don't believe in God,' and she said 'Is that so, pass me that sprinkling bottle.' His first insight. Folk were just too busy for beliefs.

Ten o'clock this Sunday morning the last day of July, a starling shrieking in a panic outside the window, a cat stalking along a branch of lime tree in a light sprinkling of rain. Samuel S sat hands over ears, eyes glued and mind rooted in a problem of spherical geometry, a little exercise to start the mental machinery and steer it away from the soul. And the telephone dimly rang under the pile of dirty laundry. It was all like climbing up to a mountain top. Tugging out the black instrument, and hear the voice of the Countess, who said she had been thinking. Would he come for morning coffee.

Samuel S set off jauntily across Vienna by tram, by foot, through the portals of palaces, down the paths of parks and between the pillars of this grey stone edifice, heels clicking across the black white squares of the marble vestibule. A quick view of himself in the mirror. Popping a last schilling admission to the elevator. A mild little penalty for a mild little luxury. Closing the antique doors, rising up three floors to her landing.

The great carved mantel over the door. A country serving girl smiling him into the drawing room. He brushed the Countess's hand lightly with his lips, just like the books said and like he felt it should be done as well. The Countess crossed her legs. That fascinating part of them just thickening behind the knees. And Samuel S stood, does one say what's this all about. Or like, as a child, at a friend's house when they sat down with the family and had soup and he wiped his mouth to get up and they asked 'Hey where are you going,' and Samuel S looked around and said, 'Home, why. Is there more.'

'You wonder why you are here, Herr S.'

'No.'

'At this ungodly hour, you must.'

'Yes, I'm lying, I wonder.'

'I like you.'

'Whoops.'

'Why do you say whoops.'

'Well Countess, I mean to say, in this world that's a pretty windy question. People say one thing and they mean another, I mean to say, remarks like that make me nervous anyway.'

'I'll come to the point. I would like to settle an income upon you. For life.'

'Wham bam, thank you mam.'

'That is not quite the expression I expected.'

'Well Christ.'

'Is that all you've got to say.'

'I know from previous experience in my life Countess that whatever I say will be the wrong thing. Especially if someone has said something I want to hear.'

'There are conditions.'

'Whoo hooo.'

'This is no joke Herr S.'

'It will be.'

'I don't quite understand.'

'You're buying me. So that every once in a while when you're feeling down you can give me a kick in the teeth.'

'I can see Herr S you like to take chunks out of the hand that feeds you. Perhaps you intend to avoid starving that way.'

'Have it your way Countess, but I would be foolish not to recognise that the joy at another's misfortune is one of the biggest doses of goodness that people gorge themselves on in this town.'

'You regard my offer as misfortune.'

'No, just the conditions which are going to make me reject it.'

'I see. How do you know until you know what they are.'

'I know human nature. There are some people who've got a kite to fly in every different wind. I've got one kite and can only fly in certain winds. So I mean to say, please do not play tennis with my heart, or which is worse my wallet, which happens to be about empty.'

'You are a most ungrateful person.'

'Perhaps.'

'And a weakie.'

'That may be true. But I will not be bought. But I'll have another cup of coffee. By the way, what are the conditions.'

Samuel S tried to remember how he got back down on the street, where he was zooming along the cobbles of the alley the Ballgasse. Somehow it was like smoking a cigarette during the great Cambrian ice age. With the feet propped up on the north pole, and blowing smoke rings around the moon. The soul bruises like the body. During this long trail of failure. Right from boyhood school days, watching the profile of the girl he loved. As she sat diagonally across the class. And afternoons following her home from school, discovering her address, and what her father did, the amount he paid for his electricity, and finding the sum a thing of mysterious beauty. Then nearly getting caught on the pebbles of their driveway spying what they ate through their window. And looking up the licence plates of her relatives, as they came to visit, who they were and what they did for a living, tracing one uncle during one Saturday, taking a bus to his town forty miles away to watch him watering his lawn. Then to say hello to this girl after a year of learning everything about her and she looked right through me as a piece of polished glass.

Samuel S stopping at a little kiosk in the wall, peering in at the deep amphibious eyes of a female face.

'Zwanzig Lucky Strike bitte.'

Tendering a twenty schilling note. Holding out a hand for the cigarettes and a handful of groschen. Flashing the eyes across the brass coloured coins. Seventy-five groschen short. Looking back into the hole.

'You have cheated me. But if it makes you feel happier.'

Samuel S, with a shrug of his shoulders said Guten Tag and with head down rambled on his way through the grey twisted medieval streets. Very nervous decision to turn down an income for life. Stretch the ethical rope some more and when I finally take the drop the noose will behead me. Got ready this morning, holding out the hands with the parted fingers and they had a glacial stillness. Matched the socks with the tie, saddle soaped the shoes, and stepped out with a military excellence and right into the floodlit nightmare. An abstract algebraic equation, C for carnality, F constant income, multiplied by a series of related variables, L laughter, T terror all to equal S for screwed.

Samuel S crossed Singerstrasse, around a

corner and into a cool shadowy alley. Sometimes you can be alive just by leaving an image of yourself on an acquaintance's mind. To the Countess, a greedy ungrateful boor. Lurking in Vienna, the great crossroads of bloods. All well mixed. None of it Irish. Could just nip in and take a look at the Habsburg Hearts. And without missing a beat of my own, straighten the shoulders again, move on. Before I break down and weep. For the buckwheat cakes smothered in maple syrup, bacon and butter. For the autumn morning, the cloudless blue sky, the curled up chestnut leaves on the lawns holding a silent scented air so many years ago.

Samuel S disappearing into a hole in the wall, under a faded old fashioned sign. Like a little walking world he was, with sewers, towns in the kidneys, forests in the lungs, lakes in the liver. Perhaps the time had come to sport the light grey shoes with the little air conditioning holes. Never underestimate human frailty. And women should take all the guff a man wants to give. The Countess slipping me her old age with a weekly retainer. And I am too coo coo to take it. But I have the price of a cup of coffee and kipferl.

Sitting down in this dim cafe. Hands folded around a cup and saucer. His long sad nose smelling up the fumes of the black swirling coffee. Breaking his kipferl and chewing. To wait for August which begins tomorrow. All the tremors of homesickness. Hearing two girls at the next table asking in broken German, then lapsing into English as they pointed to his coffee and kipferl and said we want the same as he's got. And Samuel S shot out with his Viennese to tell the confused waiter what they wanted. And this brown-haired girl turned and said to him.

'You must speak English.'

'That's right.'

'Thanks for helping us.'

'My pleasure.'

Samuel S watched her tan, clean hands, the nails bitten down, and on her finger a gold ring set with blue turquoises round a pearl. A fresh fruity fragrance from a small tan body. With the other one so fat. In this gloom a whole world flooding back, of Harvard, the furnishings of his life, a cocktail shaker, pair of shoe trees and his waistcoat pocket watch as big as a moon. And now a tingling on the skin as he heard this American voice once more, and the rustling of a map over their coffee.

'Excuse me, maybe you can help us, we're sort of lost.'

Samuel S turning slowly, in one gesture removing his hat and bowing his head. A nervous tremor in the little hill of flesh between his thumb and finger.

'But certainly.'

'We want to see the Habsburg Hearts.'

'You go out this door, turn left. Turn right. Turn left again, right again, and second left, the church which will be standing in front of you will contain the Habsburg Hearts.'

'You're American.'

'That's right.'

'Oh my God.'

'What's the matter.'

'It can't be, you're not, are you.'

'Not what.'

'Samuel S.'

'You don't know me.'

'You are. Gee, I mean I've never seen a picture of you, but somehow I wouldn't miss you anywhere. You're wondering how I know. You know a friend of my uncle who's a professor at NYU, he knows you. When we were planning our trip, he said you were one of the points of interest in Europe.'

'Despair is the word.'

'Gee, it's true, that's just, ha ha like what he said you might say. Gee Catherine, it is, it really is. I even have your address.'

'I've been evicted.'

'O gee sorry. By the way I'm Abigail and this is Catherine.'

Samuel S in the next four days waged a war of nervous steamy fortitude. A baby tiger leaping out of bed, charging across the floor to the washbasin and smashing the cold water up against the choppers and peepers, to open the lids glued closed in sleep. With one great iconoclastic happening. For the first time in five years he missed a session at the Herr Doctor's. Abigail had long hair, eyeballs white and clean, circled with lashes long dark and silky.

The first day he brought them to the

Habsburg Hearts. The third he told her that Catherine who was fat might enjoy bouncing some of it off with a horseback ride in the Prater. Abigail said he was insulting. And what kind of an American are you.

'How many kinds are there.'

'I don't know, but you don't seem like the kind of American I know.'

'Why not.'

'Well if you want to throw around insults, I know how to do that too. I mean thanks for showing us around but you know you're kind of old, you know like you should be dead or something. Like those shoes you're wearing. And the tie. I mean you're not all that thin. And that collar doesn't match your shirt, which is sort of an English affectation but is really just what a crummy English civil servant would wear.'

'You know what an English civil servant wears.'

'Yes it so happens, the kind who thinks his balls are bells to ring for tea.'

And to escape this outspoken embattled situation Samuel S suggested tea, hoping he did not chime. But fat Catherine had to be shifted. Or dynamited. Loyalties flow deep between girl friends until they want the same man. And then wham, there is no longer a bead of sweat. In which to sail friendship. And to hint and hope he whispered to Abigail.

'I would like to do dirty things to you.'

And got a look from her. Hostile without hope. Just as they were making their way quietly into the silent medieval square of the Heiligenkreuzerhof. And she stopped in front of the garden wall of the Prälatentrakt and she let him have both barrels.

'We're not so stupid as you might think. In fact you might have been around but I'm smarter than you think. We came to Europe to enlarge our area of human understanding. Only I'll be honest, also to meet guys. I know I'm not good looking enough, so I have to talk to someone weird like you. Who could be my father. Or even my uncle whose friend recommended you. At least I'm not stupid enough to overlook that you're a man. You see you made a mistake about me. I'm not a cock teaser. But you're a desperate snob. You've been looking down your nose at everybody you've ever met. Or else kissing someone's ass. You know what you are. A bully.'

Samuel S took the next few seconds to look at the shuttered windows and up into the leaves of the tree overhead to feel a few rays of warm sunlight on his face and a sentence came into his head he never thought in five years would ever get there. The Austrians are graceful of spirit. And he was an animal which hadn't got into the zoology books yet.

The fourth day. Which came up blooming full of lime tree scent and the pebbly ground was shoe sticky under the trees. The landlady suggesting they have an overture which might lead to an opera. In bed. And Samuel S said is that so Agnes, is that so, well well, you mean all the outer garments will be shed and that you will grab me and I will grab you and we will in short tangle. And Agnes's face wrinkled with secrecy said, Herr S not so loud, so someone might hear.

'Why not. Let the world know, anyway, I'm on my way to sing an aria.'

And today in this glut time of females, Samuel S sauntered out to hop the tram with a letter. He whistled for there had also been another payment from Amsterdam. He clicked his heels together reaching their rendezvous to go up to the wooded slopes of the Kahlenberg to look down over Vienna.

And here as he corrected some faults in her English she said.

'I know what you're thinking, you think I'm stupid.'

'I've said nothing.'

'Just the way you start to look away, as if you knew everything. Well I've read all the great books. And I think they all stink.'

'Please continue.'

'And I took a course on human relating. And I've got news for you. I thought that stunk too. Only I wouldn't sneer at it like you might. And all these great cathedrals around France you think are so great. I think they stink too. I'd much rather look at an honest to goodness gasoline station and get my kicks than your phoney stained glass.'

'Please continue.'

'Don't be so damned superior, with that please continue stuff.'

'This is serious. There is genuine beauty in those French cathedral towns. Or are you pulling my leg.'

'I just wouldn't be bothered pulling your leg.'

'Well I'll make a pronouncement. You're just a rootin tootin good old American college girl, who's going to grow up and be different from ma and pa. Age will teach you a lot, when things will turn out just as you thought they wouldn't.'

'So we know you're grandpa wisdom. But you've never been able to get off the college campus have you. What do you live on, handouts. You said so. And sneaking around in the libraries doing a big deal research. You're one of those guys who needs that womb of education. Why don't you go home. Back to the States. You know why you don't because the competition would close you out. They would close you out so fast boy, you wouldn't know what happened to you.'

Samuel S could not stop the tears as they rolled like boulders out of each eye. Nor lift up a sleeve to wipe them from his cheeks. Her voice seemed far away, a dim thing like waves on a shore when you lie awake and the wind is still and the sea is near. Like her lips say warmly now.

'Hey gee I'm sorry. I didn't mean to hurt your feelings like that. I'm only kidding.'

Abigail's freckled nose. Small brown eyes. Big mouth. Which opened in her face with toothful beauty. When she stood up you wanted to see the rest of her. Now she was sitting. And Samuel S was standing.

'You've bested me.'

'Hey gee.'

'You've bested me, that's alright, I asked for it. Well I'll be going.'

'Don't go.'

Samuel S flipped his cap back on his head. Waved a hand to the Herr Ober who sped wagging his black gargantuan belly to sweep up into his black folding wallet a bill Samuel S threw on the table, telling him to keep the change. The Ober, a dark cloud, smiling briefly, bowing and withdrawing. Sam S slowly pulled his sweater off the back of the chair and looked down at Abigail.

'You don't want me to go.'

'No I don't want you to go.'

'No one has ever had the courage to say that to me before. But I'm going. So long.'

His brown sweater dragged in the pebbles between the tables as Samuel S made his way away from this sunny terrace up steps to the road past the ancient church and into a hot little bus which loudly throbbed its way down the coiling highway to the shady and sleepy little town of Grinzing. In the shed across the road waited the tram back to

Vienna. On the hard arse shaped bench Samuel S sat with hands clutching each knee, fighting away a rear hollow pain. How to last twenty four hours until he saw Herr Doctor at five tomorrow. Bully. Phony. Grown soft and fat on failure instead of success. Standing alone in the middle of a great big zero.

At the tram terminus, a gleaming emporium underground, Samuel S started to cross the open space which reminded him so much of America. And dead centre of this marble floor mid the lunchtime bustling Viennese and the clanging and screeching arrival and departure of trams, he let go with one long piercing yell as the pain got him in the kidneys. His hands clutching his wallet and change purse. Holding tight to these, a miraculous path opening between the staring eyes as he made a reeling way to the gents. His pulse too fast to be counted. Splashing his face with water, mouth gobbling up air, Samuel S steadied in his panic, bending his knees, straightening his spine, wading out across the marble again and draping himself on the escalator. On the street he whispered his address and poured himself into a taxi. A porcupine he was, and all his quills were gone.

Behind his four windows, curtains drawn, Samuel S ran the bath and took his temperature. Out of his amateur but vast medical knowledge diseases were converging fast. Hard to know which would kill him first. With a trembling hand he saw the red line at one hundred and two degrees and he dropped the thermometer and it broke across his shoe. If ever there was a time to hold on. To go over to the wall to the coat hook and hang by the hands. Two minutes ticking by. Three. This is the doorway. The black one. Always left open. Step through and never come back again. Just go down without stairs and as you begin to fall, chase back through your life, shouting out in the streets for the ones you knew longest of all. They had hair and hands you touched and sat around, just sat around, and you were a child and had there been a touch which said, now don't you fret now don't you mind little boy, little boy.

A scream from the landing. Samuel S went rigid on his wrack, a pounding on his door. The desperate voice of Agnes Anxiety.

'Herr S, Herr S what are you doing. You flood out the building, the water is running down the stairs.'

'I'm dying. I'm dying.'

'Shut the water off first.'

Water flowed in a smooth cascade over the side of the tub. Samuel S standing bemused watching it make its way, a little river with a substantial current along the hall and out under his door. His personal little Danube.

Soaking down the stairs, coursing out the front archway of the building. And as it crossed the pavement, it collected a little group of people who indulged themselves in this free schadenfreude, smiling and nearly patting each other on the back. Just as Samuel S came nipping out wielding a mop, followed by a shouting Agnes Anxiety wielding another at the back of his head. The crowd laughed. He was cured. This moment, this day.

Samuel S took this Wednesday matinee vaudeville to sleep with a fear of eviction chasing him up various narrow chimneys, his churning feet dislodging lumps of soot. To rise today, Thursday and struggle past all the minutes towards five o'clock. With five minutes to go, walking along the twisting narrow shady street, pulse beating, temperature unknown. Past the grey stone church so cold inside in summer. The rays of sunlight gleaming in a thin cool mist. Stepping through a portal, between giant oaken doors. Across the cobbled courtyard past a fountain and steam smoking out from an open laundry door. The dark gloomy archway with a statue of the Blessed Virgin. A candle burning in front of her kindly face and little red lips and blue shawl.

Samuel S climbed up the forty six stone stairs, each hand touching each knee as he went. On the third landing a big door. He gave one loud rap, stepped inside this cool spaciousness and slipped his cap on a hook. With a turn of a glass knob and through another door sat Herr Doctor at his desk nodding. A newly sharpened pencil by one hand, the other resting on a yellow sheet of paper. Two large polished windows looking out over a shadowy green garden, white stone statues circled by boxwood hedges under the trees and two fat blue pigeons perched eating lilac leaves. And times a silent little girl would play there wearing white gloves.

'Good afternoon, Herr S.'

'Wow Doc. My cerebellum is ringing.'

'Please sit down.'

'I really got a tug on the medulla oblongata.'

Samuel S landed himself backwards in the soft brown leather chair worn white with elbows, backs and bottoms of patients. The tick of a large gold desk watch on Herr Doctor's desk which sounded loudly between the pauses of talk and raced ahead of one's money's worth. In the glass cabinet, seven language dictionaries, and one technical to which Samuel S often drove the Herr Doctor. On the wall diplomas from Heidelberg, Vienna, Berlin and Cambridge. Sad reminders in his own life of the dust, just dust, of his own degree. Taken one night in a sober fist and in front of a quietly smiling friend was soundly burned. A sniff of its smoke, Latin and parchment. You think it will change your brain and instead ties a tag there, seals a label over the eyes till you go stumbling towards a wall all around you, standing there unable to taste the flavour of a peach or squeal at orgasm time.

'Yes, Herr S.'

'Yesterday I got smashed. Really walked into the blades. I forgot my own rule, do not try to look big, making others feel small. I've met a girl. Just by accident. She knew about me. At least that I was the most colourful twisted personality in Europe. I thought that that gave me the upper hand. But she just flashed around and kicked me one right in the soul. I'm getting on Doc, I mean when am I going to get married and have kids, I don't want to go around a dirty old man.'

'A dirty old man, Herr S can be married with ten children.'

'Ah Doc, you stepped into it, I've got you to express an opinion.'

'Please continue Herr S.'

Samuel S pursed his lips. And Herr Doctor unpursed his, reaching with long flat fingers for a little white cigar holder. His hand freezing on the plastic under the grip of Samuel S's eyes. In this darkened room, shadows wagging on the wall from summer light tilting on the leaves out the windows. The Herr Doctor was growing thinner. Sitting there sucking on the white cigar holder without the cigar. One could draw all sorts of conclusions. Bound to be one or two misunderstandings in everybody's moments at the breast. One hopes Herr Doctor had a big ample mother. In five years I must have nearly driven him crazy. He tenses as I come in, ready to take the onslaught. Wears a calm mask as I sink in punch after punch. Some larded with pretty crazy notions, when I said Doc, the whole world should have loved me right from babyhood, instead of sneaking out from underneath the thick green group of trees to shove me around in the clearing. Then Herr Doctor slowly gets up. Walks behind me. I stop talking. He says keep talking please. I say what for. He says I'm just changing my seat. Then I know I've got him smiling. As he goes to sit and chuckle in the corner. Perhaps Herr Doctor will last after all.

'I actually cried Herr Doctor. Does that mean I cracked.'

'No Herr patient.'

'Well what should I do. I thought wait a minute. Not so fast with the rebuttal. Better beat it this time. She's got my number. Then I thought. Well that's good. If she has my number it means we can get to know each other. And I can go swinging through the trees in her jungle. But Doc it's worrying me, I'm looking for them younger and younger. What's the matter.'

'Please continue.'

'I mean to say Herr Doctor. You think getting my hands on this young bimbo that I'm trying to rub off some of her yeast mould to keep my own fermentation going. I mean what could she see in me. No money for one thing. Whoopsi doodle. Boy Doc am I off my noodle. How much longer is it before I'm cured. Before I can ask someone to marry me and have kids. I've even given up all my phony liberal feelings. I'm letting healthy prejudice sneak back into my life. Isn't that good, Doc. You must be full of them. At least I'm going to get that pleasure in before I die. I'm even thinking of having masses said for me, if they were a little cheaper.'

'Yes I see, Herr S and if you will continue please.'

'Well I was born in Pawtucket, Rhode Island in the U.S.A. on a fairly cool October day, my mother moaned with surprise as she saw her belly give rise to this yelling nine pound prize. Which grew up on what I did not know was the wrong side of the tracks. On which I got my toes continually trimmed as I stood there looking at the goodies on the other side.'

'Do not joke please.'

'Well you won't tell me anything. I'm just going back over it to see where I went wrong. And took the train to Celibacyville. I mean, Doc, this is five years I'm coming here twice a week. I lie in bed in the morning adding it all up. It's the price of an expensive car. A thing I have never owned in my whole life. I mean I could have polished it twice a week for fifty minutes. And then when someone wants to marry me and pay me as well, I run. From the biggest gravy train that ever whistled by. I want to get straightened out. And yesterday shows I am not straightened out.'

'Please don't shout, Herr S.'

'You afraid the neighbours will hear.'

'Do please continue.'

'Now answer me. Are you afraid the neighbours are going to hear.'

'No Herr S, I am not afraid the neighbours are going to hear. Do please continue. But let me warn you, you are showing all the symptoms of being cured.'

'Don't say that Doc. I'm so lonely. Really really lonely. How do I get this bimbo.'

'There is no formula.'

Samuel S pulling up his brown tightly woven socks and taking a sigh. The fan quietly whirring. Watch ticking. Out the window a whistle blowing. Belonging to the little girl in white gloves with big blue eyes and long brown hair who was allowed to make this sound when her father came home. Her tiny joy at five fifteen every day. For which she waited pushing a little baby carriage round the pebble paths, soundlessly talking to her doll.

'Maybe I've had enough for today Doc. But I want to sit here till my hour's finished.'

'It's your hour Herr S.'

'I know it's my hour. I know it annoys you. I just want to sit here and say nothing. Because I'm not getting anywhere saying things. What is it Doc, no one will let me have the good jobs, the good women. I mean look at the big international agency in this town. I mean to say, there is a big breast. Sure I want to gnaw at it. But when anyone sees me eyeing it and coming close, they say go on, we're chewing here already, go on get out of here. Those are the grabbers at life's banquet. And I'm elbowed to crawling around under the table scooping up the crumbs. Trying to avoid the heels they're slamming at my outstretched fingers for laughs.'

Samuel S stood outside the oaken doors of the Herr Doctor's building. His cap set square this five minutes to six this Thursday evening August in Vienna. Where one could walk down Goldegg Gasse feeling you'd just been laid. Here, east of Munich, Paris and Halifax Nova Scotia. Quietly loping through the back streets beneath the spire of St Stephen's as the big bell booms six. On the corners of the Kärntnerstrasse the early bird street girls taking up positions. Pale blue and pink cotton dresses, sweaters across their shoulders for late business through the cooling evening. Samuel S taking a sharp right into a short narrow grey street, entering a mausoleum interior of smoky amber coloured marble. He sat down in a booth and laid his arms out on the table, and a momentary forehead on his wrist. A waitress inclining towards this sad form.

'Herr S good evening, are you sick.'

'I am about to scramble my synapses on slivowitz. If I don't I'll end up in the blue pair of plimsolls playing the electric piano by the ice cold sea.'

The big bell was booming eight o'clock and Samuel S was standing on his table, bowing after an elaborate dance called the goof's gavotte which was an antic with the plenty use of the hips and shins. The proprietor aghast as Samuel S demonstrated American football, lesson three, the place kick using a glass of slivowitz as the ball. And asking questions of the admiring crowd, as they licked the plumy fluid from their faces, do you each have someone to love you, do you each have a cherished care. And question time was followed by a song.

Sprinkle me
With anther dust
Sprinkle me
With lime.
Sow me
Beneath the buttercups
After all
The pantomime.

There were cheers and schillings tossed on
the table. Viennese present restricting their
appreciation to clapping. But their grins
were big as Samuel S took off his jacket, and
with a cigar in one hand, his yellow suspenders wrapped around his throat and arms
spread in a cross he sang four spine soothing
Mozart arias in a row, collecting people in
from the street, jamming the doorway and
sidewalk. Just in time to see Samuel S in his
cloud of smoke raise a flag on his big toe and
demonstrate a baby's arse with his squeezed

up belly. It was mad. The less hardy turning shyly to peek from between fingers covering the eyes. And in English he announced he was going up shit's creek, with no engine, no sail, no boat and would they all wave goodbye.

Friday dawn. After the plenty troublesome Thursday. Samuel S stretched spreadeagled unconscious under his table, suspenders still entangled around his throat. A left hand holding a nun in the shape of a little black doll which made him shout out Holy Christ, and throw it across the room. The world looked yellow. Aches in the achilles' tendons, a dried alcoholic foam in the mouth. A night of tightrope walking above the abyss, and settings forth for Odessa across the frozen wastes with a collection of assorted combs to sell. Then morning. The sun creeping across his wall, a thin ray sneaking through a slit in the curtains. Struggling to the knees. Crawling squelching across the soaked carpet in the hall to wee wee. Life waiting while the liver squeezes the poison out drop by drop. And back again to the groaning horse hair mattress creeping over the little nun, a note tucked in under her white bib.

## YOU SHOULD HAVE YOUR BRAINS EXAMINED
Yours truly,
An Austrian Citizen

Samuel S lay on his bed, a vista of grey stains down his cavalry twill trousers, tips of brown shoes scuffed and torn, suspenders flapped out, broken golden wings. Staring up at the ceiling. A cracked plaster medallion, into which one would merge when it was time to go to heaven. On my back here. Nowhere. With nothing ventured. And everything lost anyway. Brains fried instead of examined. Eyes looking in instead of out. Ears barely tuned to the outside world. Agnes Anxiety lurking past the door. Wondering if I'm worth one last cold shiver. The trams' squealing stopped. Lapse to sleep. Dream of a rampaging bull rooting up daisies and roaring I'm king of the beasts. Naturally one approached to talk it over and this animal charged. Chasing me across the courtyard and into a barn where I stood trembling on top of the sweet smelling bales of hay. Whispering down to this animal puffing explosions of flame from the nostrils. Now bull can't we come to an understanding. Lead you to some grass. And the horns came whistling past his own nostrils. Waking once more. Beads of sweat on the brow. Time to wee wee. Momentous effort of the spirit, roll out. Land on the knees on the floor. Stand up, shake the head and waddle to the bathroom.

Samuel S stepping carefully between the still busy little ants in their swampy world between the hairs of his carpet. And getting out of his clothes, like taking off skin. Filling the tub brimming with steamy water. Turn off the tap. Wad up a fist full of toilet paper, and stuff it round the doorbell. Bury the telephone under the gargantuan pile of dirty laundry. Pin the window curtains together, switch on all the electric lights. Cover the armchair with the sheet, the towel. Stack the books within hand's reach. Take one tome to the bath.

Samuel S lowered himself slowly in the hot water. An ant strayed from the herd was crawling on his leg, climbing to his knee top and zooming in crazy circles there as this island of refuge sank beneath the water. The ant floating, churning madly on the surface trying to swim for shore. It was desperate. Antennae flapping in despair. And Samuel

S gently let it up on a finger. Against all instincts to kill it. It stopped on the biggest freckle of his arm chewing the mandibles for a moment. And with a flick he sent it flying to safety. Just as two sharp knocks landed on his front door.

Samuel S froze in the hot water. The landlady. Or the police. Who always want to know, if they don't arrest you, what toothpaste you're using. Another three knocks.

This is no Viennese, who take the excuse of no answer to question the neighbours about you and if they hear enough, go away satisfied. Another four knocks. The police. Smell me without a shred of respectability. To make me pay for all the drunken damage I did. And spent every penny I got from Amsterdam doing it.

'Hello in there.'

Too hot in this bath to play it cool.

Because that is the voice of Abigail. Is there any more point or need for more pain. They feel guilty rejecting you and want to come later to tell you about it at length.

'Hello in there. I know you're there. I can see the light. It's me, Abigail.'

Samuel S levering himself out of the bath, dripping across the hall. Wrapped himself in the sheet and towel laid out on his chair, and headed to the front door to avoid the shouting that spread through the paper thin walls.

'What do you want.'

'I want to talk.'

'I don't, I'm undressed.'

'I just want to say something.'

'What do you want to say.'

'I don't know yet. But I want to talk.'

'I don't want to go through the whole thing again. You beat me. That's enough.'

'That's pig headed and stupid. Why don't you face up to things.'

'Face up to what.'

'I want to get to know you.'

'Think of one reason why I should get to know you.'

'You could rest your head on my shoulder.'

Samuel S wiped the perspiration off his brow with the sheet. Take six months in Spitzbergen on an ice floe conferring with a group of Bombay dentists to find an answer to that. Or twenty seconds in Vienna.

'How old are you.'

'Old enough.'

'I'm nearly twice your age.'

'Then stop acting like a child. Open the door. I want to be friends.'

'That's the most ominous relationship in the world.'

'What's the matter with you. Are you a coward.'

'Yes, what are you.'

'I'm Jewish. Three quarters.'

'Well, I'm antisemitic, four quarters.'

'O.K. I'll improve your prejudice for you.'

Samuel S undoing the latches to the door, holding the sheet together around him with his teeth. His first visitor. Dressed in brown, a patterned silk shirt and leather skirt. A large saddle bag slung over her shoulder. And feet in deer skin ankle boots upon which she stopped half way into the musty dim sitting room and let out a high pitched whistle.

'Holy cow.'

'You wanted to come in.'

'I've read about poverty in Europe but this is really for the books. Your hallway is soaking. You look like a spook.'

'If you don't like it there's the door.'

'Don't be so touchy.'

'I don't ask people to visit me, if they do I take no responsibility for their feelings when they get here.'

'You're a charlatan. Real charlatan.'

'As I say, there's the door.'

'I have a good mind to walk right out of here. The only reason I don't is because this is the filthiest place I've ever seen. This place is really dirty. And something should be done about it. What have you got all the lights on for. And the curtains blocking out the daylight. It's three o'clock in the afternoon.'

'As far as I'm concerned it's midnight.'

'Can I sit down.'

'Sit down.'

Samuel S waddled to the bathroom. Slapped cold water on his head and slammed a comb through the matted hair, raking a jagged parting on the left slope of skull. Life had taken a new turning. Right into a little oasis. Full of foolish figs all figurative and vanishing when you reached to eat. And on top of everything else the landlady is raising snails in a glass cage in the basement. They make noise munching on the vine leaves. The Countess said she went a little strange after dark, foaming over her escargot, but seemed to come around again in the morning.

Samuel S emerged from his bathroom with the chin up, the shoulders back, sunshine beaming from the eyes. A white starched collar over a blue striped shirt. Abigail sitting with her legs crossed. Thumbing through his Guide To Banking. She looks up with brown eyes, her lips faint purple in the light.

'I'm sorry for what I said up on the Kahlenberg. I met some friends of yours and they told me you were under treatment.

If I knew, I wouldn't have said what I said.'

'People say what they want to say. And they always mean it. And then do exactly the opposite.'

'God am I embarrassed. I don't know what to say. Could we open up a window.'

'They're sealed.'

'I'm not used to these European smells.'

'This air's been here for four months and I can see no good reason to change it. Fresh air makes me sick.'

'Do you like living primitive like this.'

'No.'

'Why do you.'

'Because I haven't the money to live any other way and nobody else will clean it up.'

'You should clean it.'

'I don't feel like cleaning it.'

'Forgive me for suggesting.'

Samuel S froze. Standing solemnly by his

makeshift desk piled high with sheafs of paper. Pull in the outposts of life, the dreams, ambitions, the distant deals. So that some passing grabber swishing his scimitar doesn't lop them off. End up just being alive, the only thing that matters at all. Feel the way carefully while there are still teeth left in one's head. Beware reaching for that little flower, its stem earthed to a buried electric cable to send you flying clear across the grassy field. I reach out.

'Why did you come here.'

'To give you a lay.'

Samuel S redirected the blood back down to the toes again, where it bounced. At half past three in the afternoon. Wait for her to waver. Wait for her to wane. While I wobble and wilt.

'Hey watch that. I mean you can't say that.'

'I said it, Sam.'

'Let me sit down for a second. This situation needs thinking out.'

'Mind if I stand up.'

'No, stand up, wait let me fix you some space.'

'That's alright. I'm standing.'

'No no, just a second, you need space. Push this chair over.'

'No really that's alright.'

'Just get rid of this towel and sheet.'

'Don't go to any trouble.'

'It's no trouble.'

Samuel S dancing attendance. Unlike all the many years of putting his women under the thumb, once they had been under the rest of him. Find your own seat, open up your own door. Now a wiff of undergraduate days, the carefully drilled procedures, to look white, right and scrubbed, wearing drawers fragrant as the fir forest over one's Christmas decoration.

'Can I call you Sam.'

'Anything you like.'

'I heard you wanted a lay, Sam.'

'Let's lay off that subject for a minute.'

'Gee can we go on having a conversation like this. If you want I'll withdraw the offer.'

'Don't do that.'

'Well it's kind of undignified if I got to ask you again.'

Abigail standing belly in, chest out. A neat brown little muscle throbbing at her elbow. Sam S sinking back in his chair. Putting a hand up to the moisture seeping from his brow. In this sea green room. Used just after the war by an eye maker. Who had a bench by the window and worked swiftly through the days blowing up his neat little glass bubbles while the client sat near with his good eye glinting in the daylight as the maker took his tiny touches of colour to match up the dead with the living. The land-lady said he made hers.

'Are you going to say anything, Sam.'

'Have a piece of cake. It's stale but no mould yet. I'm covered in a cold sweat.'

'You admit everything.'

'Because I've got to come to terms with everything.'

'Boy Sam I'm going to sit down. If I have to wait while you come to terms. And you expect people not to give you a kick in the tonsils in the meantime. For your own good when are you going to wise up.'

'I've got my ways of fighting.'

'Only if you know you've got somebody you can beat.'

'I see.'

'Christ, I'm sorry I said just what I said.'

'That's why I'm here for five years. To get straightened out. So I can take those re-marks.'

'God, five years.'

'Could take another five years.'

'You can afford that.'

'I'm not affording it. I'm broke. Living on the handouts of some rich friends who can't face the pain of refusing me.'

A silence. Her brown eyes and my blue. The faint tender knuckles under the skin of her hand, taking up the cake bought in a weak sad moment for dinner and washed down with fresh clear Viennese water.

'Sam, you're a sort of honest person. Even the way you give me stale cake to eat. Guess I should adapt. I mean my whole reason for coming to Europe was to widen my area of experience. And did we walk into it. Right at Le Havre. I mean an hour off the boat heading for Paris, a French truck driver tried to lay me and Catherine. He said it would teach us about Europe. I told him his breath stank. Then he made a rude suggestion. I was sort of amused but Catherine slapped his face, he didn't know we knew so much French. Then he threw us out of the truck. I think Europeans are pretty lousy and uncouth. You've gone European. It's wrong.'

'What's right.'

'They should grow up in Europe. They think they have spiritual values. They should get wise.'

'You think so.'

'Yes, and you should problem solve. Plenty of people who are mental cripples work out of it after a while. Take me.'

'We'll take you.'

'They tried to make me a child prodigy at the piano. My parents are rich. I grew up in a green house. My mother tried to suck my father dry. But before she finished, another doll came on the scene, both trying to suck him dry, which, while they were fighting gave him a breather. I mean you want to hear all this.'

'Please continue.'

'Don't be superior.'

'I'm just listening. Continue.'

'Well I've had my problems. My mother's built like a mole. I mean she wasn't always like that but it was like she was taking the fat off my father and putting it on herself. That's an awful image to imagine. And my father said he really loves me, you know like a man really loves a woman, that kind of stuff. So I said it was abnormal. My father is a sort of good guy, you know, laughs and jokes and stuff. He really has a sense of humour. So we were able to joke. His problem is he's only half Jewish.'

Samuel S on this August Friday as the distant booming bell tolled five. Looked into these dark eyes across the table. The eye-maker would only have needed a tint of black glass in a big blob of brown. Her American behind ready to drop off with ripeness as it moves. Her gone wrong leg tanned darker and thinner than the other. A bimbo risen right up out of the deep and thick of the tourist season in Vienna. Her person slender. Shoulders small. Bury her with my fat. Delicate fingers, dark pink nails. An ocean cleanliness like autumn drift-wood on a sandy coast in Maine. Smiles die on her lips and come back to life again, just when you were sad to see them go. O bimbo. O bimbo.

'You see Sam, I'm out of Baltimore. I don't know maybe it doesn't look it, my father was raised in the back of an ice cream parlour, I mean his parents couldn't speak English, I mean if my girl friends met my grandparents my social life wouldn't be worth a gumdrop. I went to a snooty college, I mean if I didn't have money those girls would have told me where to get off I can tell you. America is riddled with snobbery. I mean you haven't been back. You don't know.'

'I know.'

'You think so. Well you should go and see how things are shaping up over there now. I mean it's masses. Real masses. I mean my eyes, I don't know how they ever got opened. But they're rolling them out of the colleges. By the thousands. You don't know. My uncle's friend said you isolate yourself. But think of all those brains cluttered with education. I got so scared. I emptied out my knowledge. Lost my virginity. That shocks you.'

'If you want to think so.'

'Boy you're difficult, but I'm talking like a waterfall to you. My uncle's friend is one guy's opinions I'm impressed by and he said you were one of the strangest items in

Europe. How you go through your daily life in Vienna and when you would get short changed you would say quietly and politely, you have cheated me, and then bow and go on your way. I thought that was really impressive. Then. You want the truth.'

'If you want to tell me.'

'Well then when I saw you, I was disappointed. First it was sort of a surprise, meeting you like that. Then as you sunk in. I thought, what. This oldfashioned guy. My father could compete with him. You realize I'm giving it to you straight from the shoulder.'

'I realize.'

'Then when I socked you with a couple of remarks and you just showed your sorrow right there in front of us, I said either this guy is pretty sick or something or else he's really special. When guys cry in America it's sort of gooey with words coming out as well.

But you weren't really crying. Just big tears rolling out independently. That's why I want to get to know you. I think you are the most interesting person I have met in Europe thus far. I think I can learn something from you.'

'Is that all.'

'Well yeah that's all. But you're a sort of uncorrupted person. I mean I don't know what I mean. But. O God. I'm a woman. And you're a man. And gee we're in Europe and we're alone. I mean doesn't that get you all excited.'

'I'm excited.'

'Well. Sam.'

'Well what.'

'Well I told you why I'm here. I'm embarrassed. Do I have to say it again. Like I said you can give me knowledge. I can give you a lay.'

'Is that all.'

'Sure that's all. What else. What did you expect.'

'I want to get married.'

'Holy cow. Are you crazy.'

'And have children.'

'Boy. Maybe we could change the subject. I mean marry. You. Jeepers. I mean you're not asking me are you. I was only talking about a lay.'

'I don't want a lay.'

'Wish you wouldn't shout. I can hear. Maybe you want me to go. I'll go.'

'I won't do anything to stop you.'

'You mean you really wouldn't stop me. Well boy you better face facts in the auction of life. And take what you can get. With a young girl like me you wouldn't stand a chance. You got grey hairs, means your reserves are running low. You can't even fall back on distinction.'

Samuel S looking at these two burning

brown eyes. Heart pounding in his chest.
The knees of her legs as she crossed them,
tightening in tiny circles of white. Deep blue
vein over the ankle bone. What is a bimbo.
Conjugate it in Latin. Conjugate it in life.
A bimbo is a small, tan and skinny thing.
With a brain you switched off like a light
when you took it to bed. Rid the mind of
knowledge when looking for pleasure. Or
start thinking and find a lot of pain.

'By the world's rules I'm a failure. But I
live here. I mind my own business. I don't
have visitors. The reason you're here is because no young ivy league guys are giving
you a tumble. You're not exactly ugly but
from the chin up no one could say you were a
prize winner. Although crazy enough I
think you're damn pretty but I know what
kids of your own age think. The smart talk
doesn't become you one bit. It's unpleasant,
cruel and bad manners.'

'Wait Sam.'

'You wait.'

'But Sam this is the kind of talk I thought would come from you. I'm glad I came. I know I was being smart saying that about laying and all. I just felt awkward coming along like this. I might have got here and found you with someone or something. But they told me you did this, went under, like a submarine or something and no one heard from you for days. I don't think you're a failure. Honest.'

'What am I.'

'Well like you said about me. People your own age might look down on you. But to me you've got maturity not even my own father has.'

'If you saw me sitting in a café just me as I am you would ignore me.'

'You're the most stubborn damn person, for Christ's sake.'

'That's right.'

'Aren't guys trying to escape marriage. You're just looking for a wife and kids now so you won't be lonely in your old age. But me, gee I want to kick the gong around some more before I get all tied up.'

Abigail sitting elbows on table. Rushing into a future. All the neat little bows tied on her past. While I have just successfully added three more painful days to my life. And when young, with my heart beating like a hummingbird, and not to know there was nectar. Too busy tripping over the tiny little customs that make people like you. Now there's nectar. With too many years of watching where I was going. Holding outstretched hands ahead, keeping off the obstacles. Knocking over the nectar.

'Boy is this a seminar, Sam. Have you got some coffee. I'll make some. What's the matter did I say something wrong.'

'No.'

'You got such a funny look. Have you got some coffee.'

'You're outraging American woman-hood.'

'What do you mean. Just because I said I'd make the coffee. Say what do you take American women for. We're not cripples you know. I'll even clean up for you here. You couldn't have cleaned this place for at least a month.'

'Three months eighteen days.'

'Wow you've got it counted.'

This Friday starting to roll away. Out of one's life. Tumbling down dusty memories of college rooms and other afternoons. A sun sinking beyond the Alps. And Samuel S said he would go and get some coffee beans around the corner. If she could loan him the money. Her eyebrows puckered, she went into a little leather purse and handed across a fifty schilling note, a smile at the corner of her lips. And as he left she asked where's the broom.

The blood throbbing in Samuel S's head. Halfway down the stairs, stopping and putting a hand up to the brow. Sometimes one had to give oneself a big bear hug of sympathy. When no one else will ever wrap arms around you like a mother. And hold you tight and safe from harm. So close now. Do I throw myself panting on her chest and locked in sweat say marry me, wash my socks, grind my coffee bean, tint my toast the lightest warmest shade of brown.

A tinkling bell ringing as he pushed through the door of the coffee shop. Where two white haired fat elderly sisters had nearly given up cheating him. And instead treated him like the managing director of a major mental institution. To which one day haplessly they might go and be glad that the Herr Direktor would give personal attention to their cases. They bow, slipping the groschen into his palm. Danke Herr Professor, danke.

Samuel S stopping in his tracks on this familiar street. A chill, an end of summer mist, a scent of Viennese winter settling with darkness. The wind grown gusty. In white apron, the candlestick maker behind his window slowly turning into a vision of Abigail with her small gymnastic body. An American girl who was going to commit a domestic chore. Just the way she said his name, Sam. Perhaps he was so behind the times that wives over there were sweating over sinks and stoves while hubby crossed his stockinged feet reading the newspaper. But his friends' American wives taught him that if he asked for an egg fried, some coffee and toast. He would get the egg. Nicely greased and neatly slipped off the pan into his lap. And coffee. Of course a generous pouring over the wrist. So died the dream to be king, alone at table, a dozen kids squabbling in another room and when the tea came with the bacon, perhaps the egg too, the wife would say, ah your nibs, is the repast to your liking, would you be wanting now a little hot cup of the tea, another rasher of the bacon. And would he, climbing back up these stairs, ever be king. To say another rasher of bacon. Ever be husband to have a wife. Be a father to have a son.

On the gloomy landing lit with feeble light from the landing below, Samuel S stood before his door, the bottom dented with kicks and the paint rutted with scratches. Inside, a present from God who at his last board meeting said gentlemen, the principles of Samuel S are to be tested today. With a comely bimbo. Who will offer Sam one piece of arse unencumbered by the usual strings. And to be preceded by a good cup of Viennese coffee. If he is not tempted to indulge the arse she will then clean up the flat and wash his dishes. If still he is steadfast, she is then to take all his dirty laundry, wash, starch and iron the bloody lot, serving him with two eggs fried with one boiled Gutsratwurst flapping in sauerkraut on a steamy plate. His stomach will easily survive this mixture according to our dieticians and if still he does not jump her, we will fly in an angel to give him apprentice character guidance, following which he shall be voted assistant to assistant treasurer of our operation, styled with the title of Saint Stubborn Sam Of The Sealed Lips And Crazy Celibacy.

Samuel S raising his arm. To put his key in the door. Twisting pushing. Into a cloud of dust. Abigail standing in the middle of the room licking the edges of her lips. Samuel

S putting the coffee beans on the sitting room table. As she turns and smiles.

'Doesn't that look better Sam. Just picking up the papers and stuff. Gee, you know it's so quiet and sort of lonely here it makes me sad. I need to wash my face now, I got so much dust over it.'

Sam S's eyes following her little fiery ass as it spread wings to fly, wagging under its animal skin to his bathroom. Two goodly tough tendons behind her knees in the smooth backs of her legs. And she came back into the room, hair combed, face washed and shining in the light.

'Sam this place isn't very soundproofed. I could hear into the next apartment. Maybe you heard me peeing.'

'There was. That music.'

'Well I'm not one of those dames who flushes the can while they pee so no one can hear them peeing. You have to pee, everybody does, so they hear you so what. Of course, it might be different if I was having a noisy crap, I might be a little embarrassed by the sound. Does it worry you.'

'My worries are silent.'

'Well mine are noisy. I was raised a free farter. Maybe I don't belch much. It interested me though which of my girl friends ever farted on a date. They would never admit it. I lost four boy friends that way, three with prospects. Can you imagine just being human, one little innocent fart and.'

'And.'

'And that's all.'

'Here's your change.'

'Oh don't bother, that's all right.'

'Here's your change.'

'God you're touchy.'

'I have conditions under which I take money and conditions under which I don't.'

'You slay me. You really do.'

Abigail leaning back against the table, propping her hands along the edge and casually staring at Samuel S's eyes. Her lower stony lip carved out of her face. Her nose set upturned between her eyes so softly brown which she thinks will make mine waver and avert. Friendship at the corner of her lips. As her eyes flicker and look down.

'You outstared me, Sam. No guy's ever been able to do that before.'

'Is that so.'

'Is it too much to ask you to address me as Abigail. You haven't once called me Abigail.'

'Abigail.'

'Not like that, after you've said something to me. Boy. I get myself into the most lousy situations.'

A moisture in Abigail's eyes. She takes two steps forward with a shambling pigeon toed awkwardness. Her wrists and hands up to her throat. Her fingers unbuttoning the top button of her blouse. And the next.

'Sam you said I was no prize winner from the chin up. How am I from the chin down.'

'Jesus Christ.'

'And here.'

'You're all right.'

'And here further down. And up.'

'All right.'

'And now. How am I all over. A surprise package.'

'Let me sit down.'

'Sam. We're really going to do it.'

'No we're not. Wait a minute. You forgot what I said about marriage.'

'We can't worry about that now. Look at me from the chin down. Really, how am I.'

'Something.'

'Really.'

'To remember. Right into old age. And later in the hereafter.'

'You've got a sense Sam of humour I never thought you had.'

'Humorous of you. To think so.'

'Take off your clothes Sam.'

'Dance.'

'Sure.'

Little sounds of a new world inside the threadbare crimson curtains of this sea green room. With night closed down on Vienna. The soft stone colours of streets between the big ghosty friendless shadows of buildings. To go walking at this time shielded from eyes. Figures disappearing from pavements to their soup, bratwurst and chunks of bread. And you keep moving listening to the click of the heels, because stop and you might die right there. Without ceremony or tears. And be parcelled up and deposited in the loamy soil of the Zentral Friedhof with an epitaph.

He was
If nothing
A Nice guy.

Samuel S took off his clothes. She said as she followed him into bed that he was not hairy. He put his arms around her elfin body and squeezed. She said you're stronger than I thought. Rolling on top of her the horse-hair creaked and creaked again when she lay on top of him. And looked him in the eye.

'You're not going to do anything are you.'

'No.'

Abigail creeping inches away from this walrus. And stretched on her back staring up at the ceiling.

'You must be the worst rat who ever lived. You don't know what that can do to a girl.'

'I know.'

Abigail turning, eyelids tightening over the big gleaming blackness centre of her eyes. Merest tremble of her lip.

'You couldn't.'

'You don't know what screwing without a future can do to me.'

Abigail shifting upon her elbows. Her eyes widening. Slight shake of her head and long whitish breasts swinging above her brown belly.

'I can't marry you. What would a girl like me do for maybe the thirty or forty years after you were dead. But I would stay right here with you screwing for two whole months. And I wouldn't mind making coffee and things like that every once in a while. Holy cow. What am I telling you. I mean God who do you think you are, like if you could fart in B flat or something.'

'That's right.'

Abigail's ears twitching. Samuel S lifting

the covers with an elbow and letting go with a neat semiquaver.

'Wow. You're a tuning fork. No kidding that was B flat, Sam. You may think that's just funny but that's impressive.'

'Marry me and I'll give you an organ recital.'

'I know you could. I believe you. But why can't you just be content with getting what you're getting. What I'm offering. Haven't I got one of the best bodies you've ever seen. While you were getting the coffee I took off what I had underneath so I could show you fast all at once. Isn't it the cat's meow.'

'I'm panting.'

'Well don't think I'm going to stick around.'

'Don't.'

'I won't don't worry.'

'For you this is just a tourist itinerary. For

me it's a steam shovel full of sod flipped on my coffin.'

Abigail crouching up on her hands and knees and her brown hair dropping forward on her cheeks. Hardened little nipples wagging on her chest. The brief feel of one against the eye could break all resolve.

'Sam. Listen. I'll be honest. It's asking me to sign up with a loser when I've still got maybe three or four years to find a boy or guy who's better off than I am or somebody who's made out as good as my father. Besides, I like sleeping some more with different guys. I mean it's no kidding. Maybe they all can't use their ass holes like trombones but its funny and interesting with all the different tools you come across. Some curve into left field, some into right. Crazy the way no two tools are the same. The end is like different kinds of fruits, some like an apple, ones like pears, yours is like a cherry. Some cherry. No kidding. I mean guys don't know. They think they're debasing me. I got news for them. My interest is highly scientific biological. I could tell them things. Gee listen to me. A seminar again. Come on. Yours goes into centre field. First one I ever saw did that. You can never tell the direction or the real size till it's hard. Let's not waste it like this. How about it. Huh. I'll blow. Warm air, ha ha, in your ear.'

'No one is saying you can't make it stand up and sing.'

'I've come all the way to Europe to get really laid, Sam.'

'I came all the way to Europe to get really cured.'

'Couldn't I cure you.'

'I've put three docs out of action already trying to cure me.'

'Haven't I got big but dainty breasts.'

'And my present doc is ready to sail for Hungary any day down the Danube.'

'To hell with you. I'm going to sleep. Good night.'

Samuel S turned on his arm and thought he could hear the plop of tears on the sheet. Reaching out to take a handful of her arse she pushed his hand away. To leave hour after hour tolling a sad bell in the distance. To screw her is to let her get away for ever. Her head on the pillow, her nose stuck between fingers, each jointed with its own shape and curve, all flexible like amber beads. Brown hair flowing down her back. Smooth skin beneath her eyes. Lips parted. Her breath smells of cooked cabbage. She doesn't know that a woman's shyness makes you do all sorts of amazing things. Even to screwing her.

Samuel S fell asleep like the car passing, hearing it long before it arrives and long after it goes, whirring away on the lonely cobbled road. And dreaming of tip-toeing across white fluffy clouds high over a rough blue sea, to come to a fence, a gigantic bean stalk woven in the steel mesh. Trying to climb up it and on top getting caught on a wire. Falling and the wire ripping back a thick strip of flesh from the thigh.

Samuel S awake with a scream, tearing off the blankets, his hand shooting down his leg to grab in a thatch of hair and pull it away from the pain. A ring of bleeding teeth marks deep in the flesh.

'What the hell are you doing.'

'Biting you.'

'You crazy.'

'Yes.'

'Blood all over my leg.'

'Don't worry you won't die.'

'Jesus Christ you're not safe.'

Samuel S gliding from the bed. Casting a glance behind at this werewolf and vampire, eyes glittering from a hood of bedcovers. The hurried movement one finds suddenly in the knees along with a slight trembling trying to stand still. Rivulet of blood right to the ankle bone. Herr Doctor will have to consult his occult encyclopaedia for this. While I catch a case of hydrophobia and go bouncing into heaven with a convulsive seizure. With an insight flashing just above the pearly gates. Refuse to screw and a woman will chew off your leg.

Four forty six a.m. Outside down on the coolly awaking street trucks rumbling by with vegetables for the Naschmarkt. The whirr, clang and flash of blue of the first tram switching tracks. This half hour till dawn. Sitting in a chair, Samuel S wrapped in a sheet. Looking across this yellow lit room. Switch the light off. Hear the heave of

Abigail's little body flinging herself on her side.

'O.K. I bit you. Don't you ever have the urge to bite. Maybe you're too educated. Well I'm primitive. Maybe I just like the taste of blood. Besides you should have fucked me.'

'I'm finished screwing for screwing's sake.'

'Bully for you. What did you take your clothes off for. You got a dirty mind.'

'You're right. I have.'

'Well I really think so. O Christ. O God. O Jeroboam. O Sid. O Joe. All you good guilty college guys I've been turning my nose up at. I mean you think you're going to get a dose of maturity. Boy. You talk about insights. You gave me one. I prefer a guy who can't get it hard to a guy who won't even use it. I've got a headache. I need an aspirin.'

'I'll get you one.'

'Don't bother. The pain's fine.'

Samuel S's big pocket watch ticking loudly on the table. Grey light creeping down over the buildings. Trams grinding by. Vienna goes to work. Little satchels over shoulders. Stepping out of doorways, huddling down streets, collecting on the corners, waiting. A prayer for all the silent little children who commit suicide in Austria. A handclap for matronly Viennese women with their young boys. And a blast of B flat for me. With a bimbo. Who's older than I'll ever be.

A creak of the horsehair. Abigail's little face a white oval in her dark hair turning towards him. Her legs tucked up to make a ball in the bed.

'Sam. What's the matter with you. Could you tell me. I say all kinds of things but it's like bouncing bricks off an iceberg. I don't have any confidence at all. This is going to sound crazy but I like you. But do you really believe what you think. Because that's the way a woman thinks. I mean Christ what do I think. At this stage six o'clock in the morning. Catherine back at the hotel who'll be itching to know every detail. I guess you already assumed because I've been so outspoken that I'll go talking about you to the outside world. That what you think.'

'No.'

'Ho hum. Tell me did you ever crap on an airplane.'

'No.'

'On a plane zooming about twenty thousand feet or something in the air and you think wow if it ever dropped you wouldn't want to be somewhere down there underneath quietly listening to background music. I'm nuts. Holy God. How's the wound. Blood's showing right through the sheet. I feel awful. I didn't know I bit that deep. Could I make a bandage or something. Didn't brush my teeth since yesterday breakfast is that bad.'

Abigail slowly climbing from the blankets. Putting an uncertain foot on the floor. Stepping towards Samuel S wrapped stoic in his sheet, his left hand holding the stained thin cotton fabric pressed against his thigh. Abigail gently lifting back the sheet from his whitish freckled leg.

'Can I see. My teeth do that.'

'Your teeth did that.'

'God am I sorry. Please at least let me take care of it.'

Abigail staring at the wound. Her hands rushing up to her face. Her narrow back bending to make a line of white bumps down her spine. A long groan, her face in pain. A shiver in Samuel S. Abigail slumped to her knees. Little person crumpled up so small.

'Sam can you help me. I need help. The

first thing that ever happened to me was with my dog. I did it with my dog. I got bitten. You ought to know, has that doomed me.'

Icy fingers clutching at Samuel S, haunting filaments, the big jelly fish in the ocean of fears the world wraps round you when the gradient is down, and down. And you've got to get up and run. As fast as you can go. Out across the landing, down the steps, along the strasse. Grab two litres of sour milk to set the stomach right. Say goodbye to the landlady's snails, goodbye to the Countess, goodbye goodbye to weirdery everywhere. Who's the doctor, who's the patient. Where's the willies. They're here. Willies everywhere.

> Open wide
> Where the willies are
> Shut the gate
> After they
> Are gone

If they turn
To come back again
Run run.

'Sam aren't you going to talk. You embarrassed or something. O God, excuse me for laughing, I bit other guys. It worries me but sometimes it was so funny I was convulsed. You look worried.'

'I'm worried.'

'Should I be worried.'

'I don't know.'

'I don't feel sick but I guess I am.'

Footsteps passing on the landing. Shuffling across. Herr Professor from upstairs. Out to get his early morning blocks of ice. Who said as they met once in the hall that he was experimenting. With an ice that would never melt. Like the match that would always light. And did Herr S understand science, that he heard from the Hausfrau that he was educated at Harvard. And Herr Professor said the blocks of ordinary ice were only a control he used in the experiment. Did Herr S understand. Herr S understood. As the Professor would go, footsteps fainter and fainter up to the attic where he had skidded into senility but spoke impeccable Greek. And once or twice in that language they kicked around a few imponderables on the landing. Which had the Hausfrau who could get no inkling hissing for quiet out a crack in her door.

'I wrote my father letters from college while I was in the nude and I told him that's the way I was. In the nude. I don't know I still feel absolutely normal. Do you. Sam.'

'I don't know.'

'Why you wrapping up like that. Afraid I might bite it on you.'

'Could be that I'm not feeling like being an entree after your hors d'oeuvres.'

'You have the mind of a child, you know that.'

'I know.'

'You mean you're content with that.'

'I'm content.'

'I think you're a voyeur too.'

'That could be.'

'Being a child and voyeur doesn't look good at your age. I don't know why I'm wasting time lecturing you. Except if nothing else is resulting from this relationship we might just as well spread around the advice.'

'The poison.'

'Well sure. Hey what do you mean poison.'

'That's what you're splashing at me.'

'Let's change the subject, holy cow. But I wish I knew what angle you look at life from.'

Samuel S reaching under his thigh to brush away a drop of blood. The same reddened knuckle put to his nose to wipe away a bead of cooled sweat. Sitting, a sphinx, head patient, calcified lover. Confidant of inventors, rich blonde countesses, and naked seminar conducting bimboes. Grown gargantuan with pride sadly proved with principles. Fanned into the world's most august failure. To lead a parade of those abject across the Alps, through Munich past Paris and on a raft to set sail from Brest and land on the shore of New Jersey a little left of Staten Island and there dedicate and erect a hall of failure surrounded by catkins in the nearest swamp. A chapel where his friends could come from foreign cities to sit at his feet apologizing for their worldly riches and success.

'What are you thinking all silent Sam.'

'I was thinking I was chairman of a billion dollar bank.'

'What if I came in asking for a loan.'

'I'd give it you.'

'You would. Gee how is this going to end Sam.'

'It's going to that's all.'

'I feel all switched around now. Don't you have any advice to give me.'

'What do you want to hear.'

'Well if there's something wrong. With me.'

'What I say doesn't matter.'

Abigail rising to her feet. Two hands knotted in fists at her thighs. The soft dark brown curly hairs under her belly, a little pillow where one might lay one's head.

'You pompous prick. And don't you ever dare tell anybody what I told you.'

'You think it's so worth telling.'

'Just don't ever tell anyone that's all. I know the kind of crap these psychiatrists like to hear. They revel in it. They got dirty minds.'

'You think so.'

'I think so.'

'A minute ago you were asking for help.'

'That's right. But you can't give it. You take but you can't give. I scare you, don't I. Well if you want news, you're beginning to scare me. I might be nuts but you're a monster. You don't know a thing about me. Not a thing. Get that straight. Have you got it straight.'

'I've got it straight.'

'Just so long as you have. And you think something's gone on with my father.'

'I've said nothing. I've got it straight, I don't know a thing about you.'

'That's right. You don't. Because my father and I love each other. O God Sam. O God. Please, have you got anything to drink. Please.'

Samuel S in his sheet going to the bathroom. Stepping over four little ants reconnoitring around a crumb of bratwurst chewed sixteen less merry days ago while wallowing in the bath. They go pulling together to store up for winter. While I reach behind this pedestal of the washbasin, feeling as one's hand goes down through the cast iron hole that a snake is going to strike.

Abigail reaching out for the glass of whisky, her hand touching his. Putting the tumbler to her lips and drinking in a gulp. Holding out the glass for more. Samuel S bending his wrist over the bottle and pouring. Her head thrown back. The whisky gone. The morning light sparkling in her tears.

Samuel S sitting one bellied, forty times busted. Abigail leaning across, two slender breasts waving, to push the empty glass on the table. Wide dark eyebrows raised, lips tightened, hand momentarily put to twist a strand of her hair round a finger. And thighs together, she moved off the bed. Picking her underwear out of her saddle bag. Shaking the flimsy black silk. Turning her head to Samuel S.

'Don't watch me dressing.'

Nearby factory siren blowing. Seven o'clock when the strange half poisonous half perfumed smell seeped through his sealed windows. Boiler fires stoked, smokestacks awake. Abigail standing in her deer skin shoes at his corroded mirror pulling a comb through her hair. She takes up her bag, moves the strap across her shoulder and near a churning shaft of sunlight dust, stands in the doorway.

'Goodbye. And I regret about the wound.'

'You know how to take the tram.'

'I know. Einmal zur Oper, bitte.'

'Sehr gut.'

'Wish there was little more of this sunshine in this situation. I'll send you a post-card. You know. O forget it. Goodbye.'

In his kitchen Samuel S boiled up a cup of coffee. Elbows propped on the wooden chopping board near the stove. A dream of where he would be slicing garlic and onions and hammering tenderness into horsemeat. Like his principles all hammered into failure. Letting go what one wants too much to keep. Always too late to say stay. Would only make her heart snap shut in my face. In the old days there were friends to visit on a Saturday afternoon to keep warm from the world.

> Instead of dancing
> Lonely
> Wearing only
> The cobra skin belt
> And the camel hair
> Pulse warmers.

Monday cool, clouds high, the light sunny. With a memory of snuggling against her solid little arse. Samuel S took a bath of warm waters ascending the chest and dipping in and out of the ear lobes. And after careful cleansing and drying of his wound, he set forth east for three miles along the course of the Wein River where it flowed unseen in its concrete bed and disappeared under the Naschmarkt. By the Opera through the crowded Kärntnerstrasse. He took a coffee and kipferl in the cafe where he met Abigail.

At three o'clock he phoned the Countess. She said she was too exhausted and strained for a confrontation. Samuel S said he would phone precisely at this time again. Next year. And as the church bells tolled four he boarded the 71 tram where it circled around the philosopher named streets. From the tram window the flashing sight through the

Belvedere Garten gate of the white paths and neat hedges round the flat green grass. He should have planted a seed in Abigail.

Tuesday this ninth of August Samuel S entering Herr Doctor's courtyard. A quiet rain falling which began yesterday afternoon as he wandered through the Zentral Friedhof. A solemn afternoon, always in sight of the distant dome of the crematorium. And walking the empty paths of the Jewish section, past the ruined church, bullet chipped walls, and shell craters on the smooth granite headstones. While it rained watching two women building a wall, mixing cement, laying bricks with sleeves rolled up on tan powerful arms, licking raindrops from their noses. A wife like that could move a mountain. And break your neck. And then on All Souls Day buy flowers from the crescent of stalls outside the massive gate to put them on your grave. To rest finally in this square mile of death, where the bushes were grown over the graves and the little wooden crosses rotted away to leave nothing at all. How does one ever learn to take off an enemy's underwear and sell it back to him thread by thread.

Samuel S tipping his cap passing the Herr Doctor's Hausbesorger peering from her little window, a cat in her arms, rubbing her finger on its squat nose between its big yellow eyes. To the statue of the Blessed Virgin at the bottom of the stairs, he said gesundheit and flipped his cap again and heard a clicking disapproving tongue from a face peeking out the courtyard's laundry door. Vienna was built of stone with eyes laid between.

In front of Herr Doctor's door to pause a moment. One big dream carried safely here trailing a sizzling fuse. An explosive insight. On the platform of the Nordbahnhof. As good a place for a dream as any. Give Herr

Doctor, standing at his window looking into the back garden, the willies.

'What's up Doc. Why you standing. Usually you're sitting at your desk. Someone spying on you from across the garden. Big purge of doctors who overcharge in Vienna, I hear.'

'Do sit down Herr S.'

'Sure Doc. I've really got some things for you today. Which have been zinging around the pons varoli since Saturday, and they're crowding right up the ninth and fifth nerves. You must remember those, the ones you expose in the dogfish. Well. It's happened. I just turned down my first free piece of ass with no strings attached. Just dangling there in front of me for one whole night. You listening Doc. And I've also got a big dream to tell you. Hey, you look worried. You ought to smoke a cigar. I mean you can afford it out of fees.'

'Herr S.'

'Was ist Doc.'

'I would prefer if you did not speak German to me. Herr patient.'

'Hold it, something's wrong Doc.'

'Yes Herr patient.'

'Maybe you heard I'm organizing a union of patients for lower fees. Heh heh.'

'What I'm going to tell you Herr patient is something I do not want you to misunderstand. You are an extremely intelligent man and I do not think you will.'

'I'm listening Herr Doctor. What's your problem.'

'Herr S you are driving me nuts.'

'Whoa.'

'A sign that you are well and truly cured.'

'Wait Doc.'

'Please. If you will. This hour is free with my compliments. Therefore I should like to continue.'

'What are you going to do with all my money you've got.'

'Herr S you well know over these five years my fees have gone up and yours has not.'

'True. But what Doc do you do with the money.'

'Herr patient may I suggest that that is my business.'

'Well it keeps me awake and agonizes me and if I knew it would help that's all.'

'I invest it.'

'In what.'

'Please Herr S, I've answered your question.'

'No you haven't.'

'What is the difference what it's invested in.'

'Well if it makes no difference why not tell me.'

'I invest it in manufacturing.'

'Manufacturing what.'

'Chemical products.'

'What chemical products.'

'I think perhaps our session is over Herr S.'

'No it isn't. I want to know what you've put my money in. Or I'm sitting right here until I do.'

'Very well Herr S. I invest in oral contraception and munitions.'

'O.K.'

'Does it answer your question.'

'Yup.'

'I am glad to hear that.'

'Well Doc you're really going to miss my shooting the shit to you. You're smart to kick me out into the cold world. Three more months of me and you would be sitting there a salt pillar.'

'Perhaps Herr S.'

Samuel S in his chair his hands spread out on the leather arms. While still here he was here forever. And all the silence now listening to the Herr Doctor's watch tick costs nothing at all. To go to sleep. While he is still there on the other side of the desk. A punching bag. A pillar of salt. To break my fists. A last hour after hundreds. And this one free. Like a beer back in the States, it's on the house, buddy. The glass that tastes best of all. For which you almost wait through all the others. And this final session given me the biggest insight of all. That if ever I'm cured I will never know it.

'So long Doc.'

'Goodbye Herr S.'

Samuel S launching himself upright. Herr Doctor standing. Behind him the window and below the sound of the little girl blowing her whistle. Herr Doctor rubbing his thumb in his fingers. Means he wants to shake hands. Against my principles. All the feelings I've hurt. To begin things with a handshake when you know later they will be crawling up to clutch you around the neck.

'Doc, one thing before I go out this door the last time. Do you ever think you'll be cured.'

'No Herr S.'

'Doc you won't believe this but you're a good guy. Thanks anyway for what you tried to do.'

'Herr S I will voluntarily express an opinion. You are a strange person. And it is a pity you would turn me into a pillar of salt, for I could listen to you much longer.'

On the street all bravery dying in the chill of summer rain landing on the heart. A throb in the emblem of teeth on the thigh. Tears welling in Samuel S's eyes. Moving slowly away. Forty steps he counted and in a great heave of the spirit he broke. Shoulders folded like wings and clutching his face with hands he lay against the corner of a doorway.

Dream untold. Of seeing Abigail and Catherine off on a train. Helping to pile their luggage. Like a gentleman. And then he got Catherine. All her big fat piece of her. Slamming it in all the way to the horizon. And then turning. To see entering the station. Two figures. One dark, one light. One the Countess the other, Herr Doctor. And as they passed, porters lugging their white elegant cases, he was crushed up against the train's wheels. And then he was dying and you think that you don't want your friends to know you died screaming in pain but that you were brave, kept your mouth shut and said nothing at all.

> Like
> A summer fly
> Waltzes out
> And wobbles
> In the winter.

J. P. Donleavy

# The Onion Eaters

On a grey cold day in a damp gloomy city Clayton Claw
Cleaver Clementine of The Three Glands descended
directly in the male line with this medical rarity intact
sets off westwards to take up residence in the vast haunted
edifice of Charnel Castle. Clementine, a polite unknown
unsung product of the new world and recently recovered
by a miraculous cure from a long decline, alights at an
empty crossroads. Standing lonely on its windswept
hillside the great turrets and battlements rear in the sky.
Clementine destitute but for his monstrous dog Elmer
and a collection of toothbrushes enters this ancient stone
fortress. Bedevilled by rats and rotted floors Clementine
stands unbelieving as an unpaid staff assembles out of
the woodwork and guests appear barefaced on the tiles
of the great hall with their equipment of audiometers,
waterpipes, onions and other venomous reptiles. Bills
run up, debts accumulate, confusion mounts and the
Army of Insurrection threatens while the definition of
clarity is ringingly declared as 'that force given to a fist
sent in the direction of a face that when hit has no
trouble seeing stars'.

Madness triumphs over love, beasts over man, chaos over
reason and for the moment life over death.

# A Fairy Tale of New York

'Fantastically inventive . . . madly funny. He is an
original and almost irresistible writer' – *Sunday Times*

'Cornelius Christian is J. P. Donleavy's new hero, person,
protagonist, figure-head, creature. He struts and weaves
and shrugs and punches his way through the pages of
*A Fairy Tale of New York*. I think he is Mr Donleavy's
best piece of man-making since Sebastian Dangerfield
in the good old ginger days. The book is fast, funny
and addictive' – Robert Nye in the *Guardian*

'Irony, farce, satire and lyric' – *Spectator*

J. P. Donleavy

# A Singular Man

His giant mausoleum abuilding, George Smith, the
mysterious man of money, lives in a world rampant
with mischief, of chiselers and cheats. Having
sidestepped slowly away down the little alleys of success
he tiptoes through a luxurious, lonely life between a
dictatorial Negress housekeeper and two secretaries,
one of whom, Sally Tomson, the gay wild and willing
beauty, he falls in love with.

'George Smith is such a man as Manhattan's subway
millions have dreamed of being' – *Time Magazine*

# The Unexpurgated Code

*A Complete Manual of Survival and Manners*

Comprising:
Social Climbing
Extinctions and Mortalities
Vilenesses Various
The Pursuit of Comfortable Habits
Perils and Precautions and
Mischiefs and Memorabilia

No stone is left unturned in this ruthless guide to social
etiquette, no left turn unstoned. Whether you're puzzled
by the meaning of life or merely lacking the basic human
decencies, rest assured you can reach the top. For
Donleavy shows you how!

J. P. Donleavy

## Meet My Maker The Mad Molecule

'In this book of short pieces Donleavy has given us the lyric poems to go with his epics. They are almost all elegies – sad songs of decayed hope, bitter little jitterbuggings of an exasperated soul, with barracuda bites of lacerating humour to bring blood-red into the grey of fate. These stories and sketches move between Europe and America, New York and Dublin and London. America is always the spoiled Paradise, the land of curdled milk and maggoty honey. The place that used to get you in the end, but that now does it in the beginning' – *Newsweek*

'The stories are swift, imaginative, beautiful, and funny, and no contemporary writer is better than J. P. Donleavy at his best' – *New Yorker*

A collection of short stories and sketches which were published between 1954 and 1964 in leading English and American papers and magazines. First published in book form in the United States in 1964, England 1965.

J. P. Donleavy

## The Ginger Man

'In the person of *The Ginger Man*, Sebastian
Dangerfield, Donleavy created one of the most
outrageous scoundrels in contemporary fiction, a
whoring, boozing young wastrel who sponges off his
friends and beats his wife and girl friends. Donleavy
then turns the moral universe on its head by making the
reader love Dangerfield for his killer instinct, flamboyant
charm, wit, flashing generosity – and above all for his
wild, fierce, two-handed grab for every precious second
of life' – *Time Magazine*

'No one who encounters him will forget Sebastian
Dangerfield' – *New York Herald Tribune*

## The Beastly Beatitudes of Balthazar B

Balthazar B is the world's last shy elegant young man.
Born to riches in Paris and raised in lonely splendour,
his life spreads to prep school in England. There he is
befriended by the world's most beatific sinner, the noble
little Beefy. And in holidays spent in Paris Balthazar B
falls upon love and sorrow with his beautiful governess
Miss Hortense, to lose her and live out lonely London
years, waking finally to the green sunshine of Ireland
and Trinity College. Here, reunited with Beefy, he is
swept away to the high and low life of Dublin until
their university careers are brought to an inglorious end.
They return to London, there to take their tricky steps
into marriage, Beefy in search of riches, Balthazar in
search of love.

'Donleavy at his best, eloquent, roguish and at last at
one with his world and the terrible sadness it contains' –
*Newsweek*

Plays by J. P. Donleavy
Published in one volume:

# The Ginger Man

Presented at the Fortune Theatre, London, in 1959.
Presented at The Orpheum Theatre, New York, in 1963.

Published in the United States and in England in 1961,
with an introduction by the author, *What They
Did in Dublin*, an account of the play's transfer to
Dublin where it was made to close.

# Fairy Tales of New York

Presented at the Pembroke Theatre, Croydon, England,
in December 1960 and then transferred to the Comedy
Theatre, London, in January 1961. Winner of the
*Evening Standard* 'Most Promising Playwright of the
Year' Award in 1960.

Published in the United States and in England in 1961.

# A Singular Man

Presented at the Cambridge Arts Theatre, Cambridge,
England, in October 1964 and at the Comedy Theatre,
London, later that month.

Published in England in 1965.

and

# The Saddest Summer of Samuel S

J. P. Donleavy

# The Destinies of Darcy Dancer, Gentleman

His future is disastrous, his present indecent, his past divine. He is Darcy Dancer, scion of the gentry, youthful squire of Andromeda Park and rider of horses and housekeepers to hounds and to bed. His adventures as a vagabond across country and in bohemian Dublin in search of the lost glories of his youth are ferociously comic, hilariously sad.

And what else did you expect from the great Donleavy? This is one of his finest novels, brim-full of zest and life.

'Truly and uniquely life-affirming . . . an almost magically potent blend of the vulgar and the elegant, the grotesque and the lyrical, the archaic and the lewdly up-to-date' – *Listener*

'Tender, sexy and tough by turn, it is always easy, conversational, constantly ruffled by surprises . . . [it] is one of his most ambitious odysseys and his most enjoyable yet' – *Vogue*

PENGUIN BOOKS

# BROTHER IN THE LAND

Danny is one of the lucky ones, a survivor, one of those who have come through a nuclear holocaust alive. But the world he knew, his home town of Shipley, has gone sour in more ways than one. The harsh law of survival rules in this now dangerous land and only those who can find uncontaminated food and water will live. Things aren't as bad as they might be for Danny and his young brother, Ben, because their father owned a grocery store. But who knows how long they will be able to defend their food stocks against the starving attackers outside?

In the midst of this terrible struggle for life, Danny meets a girl called Kim. Tough, streetwise, she trusts no one. Yet it is through Kim that Danny becomes aware of something that remains despite the bombs, despite the hunger, despite the cold – something that makes him want to go on living . . .

Robert Swindells was born in Bradford in 1939, the eldest of five children. He was a clerk, an engineer and a printer until 1969, when he entered college to train as a teacher. In 1980 he gave up teaching to write full time. He is married with two daughters, now grown up, and lives in Bradford. He is a much-acclaimed writer for children and a member of his local Peace Movement group. *Brother in the Land* is a winner of The Other Award and the 1984 Children's Book Award.

**+ *Plus* ▶**